There's a Duck in My Closet!

written by John Trent, Ph.D.

illustrated by Judy Love

Tommy NELSON

Thomas Nelson, Inc.

Nashville

*To all of us—young and old—
who have pulled the covers up over our heads at times.
And to my precious wife, Cindy, who loves away Kari and Laura's fears
. . . and mine as well.*
—JOHN TRENT

*To the art moms—
in appreciation of all their guidance and encouragement.
And to John and my photographer, Evelyn,
a very special thank you.*
—JUDY LOVE

There's a Duck in My Closet

Copyright © 1993 by John Trent for text.
Copyright © 1993 by Judy Love for illustrations.

All rights reserved.
No portion of this book may be reproduced in any form without the written
permission from the publisher, except for brief excerpts in magazine reviews.

Managing Editor: Laura Minchew
Project Editor: Brenda Ward

Library of Congress Cataloging-in-Publication Data.

Trent, John T.
  There's a duck in my closet/John Trent; illustrated by Judy Love.
    p. cm.
  Summary: A little boy is afraid of his closet at night until he discovers
that a variety of animals live in it and come out at night to play.
  ISBN 0–8499–1037–4 (hardcover)
  ISBN 0–8499–5809–1 (tradepaper)
  [1. Bedtime—fiction. 2. Sleep—fiction. 3. Fear—fiction. 4. Animals—
fiction. 5. Stories in rhyme.]
  I. Love, Judy, 1953– ill. II. Title.
P8.3.T693Th   1993
[E]—dc20   93–15707
                                                          CIP
                                                          AC

Printed in the United States of America

97 98 99 00 01 LBM 9 8 7 6 5 4 3 2 1

A Message to Parents

Childhood fears are common, normal, and frustrating. They can turn a happy "good night" into an hour-long battle to go to bed. They can wake a child up in tears and keep parents up even later trying to decide what to do about them.

During the years I've counseled families, I've noticed that for many children the focus of their uncomfortable feelings is their closet. While it may be well organized, filled with toys, and no source of alarm during the day, at night a child's closet can become a scary, foreboding place.

As one way of helping to calm nighttime jitters, I've written this book with three underlying assumptions in mind. First, there's the need to honestly face our fears. Many of us, either as children or adults, have learned to talk *around* issues rather than face them. After reading this story, ask your child, "Have you ever felt afraid at night?" Listen to his or her answer with acceptance. Sometimes discussing a story can give you a window into your child's fearful feelings.

Second, *There's a Duck in My Closet!* helps to "reframe" a negative into a positive. Instead of a closet's being a dark, foreboding place in a child's imagination, it can become his or her own personal zoo!

And third, being able to laugh about something that causes us to fear can also help us face our concerns in a healthier way. In a recent study, four-year-olds laughed an average of almost seventy times a day! Their parents, particularly those in their thirties and forties, laughed *three to four* times a day! Many of our homes need more laughter to help bring warmth and security to our children.

There's a Duck in My Closet! has become a special story for our daughters, Kari and Laura. It has turned the closets in the Trent home into friendly, safe places instead of scary ones. I pray that the warm, fuzzy animals in this book will be an encouragement to your loved ones as well. May the promise of Proverbs 3:24 be true in your child's life.

John Trent, Ph.D.
President
Encouraging Words

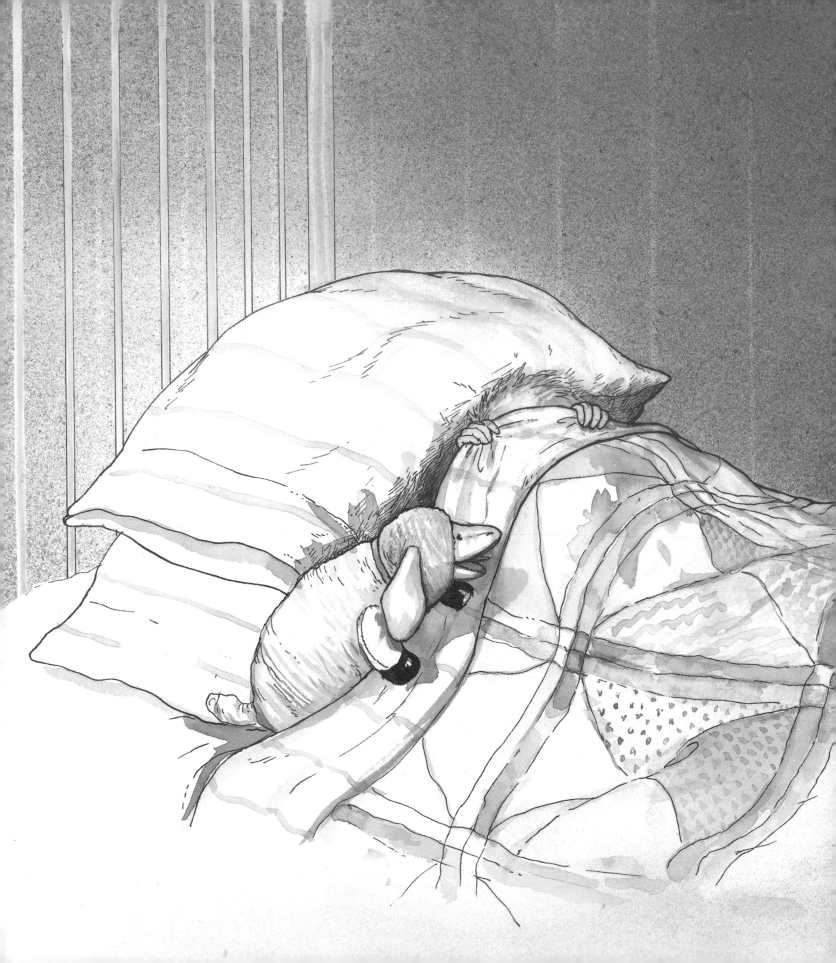

There used to be something that filled me with dread . . .
That made me pull covers up over my head.
It's my closet! That place where I keep all my clothes
Hung up on hangers, with my shoes in neat rows.

I don't mind my closet as long as it's day . . .
But turn out the lights, and it scares me away.
But that was before I found out by surprise . . .

There's a duck in my closet!
Right in front of my eyes!

There are actually *two* ducks that live there, you see,
Two ducks that come out when they think I'm asleep.
These ducks, they don't bite me or tickle my knees,
They just snuggle up by me and Oscar, my sheep.

But how did they get there? you might want to know.
They were let in by *pandas*, who sleep by my toes.
You see, in my closet there are two pandas, too,
Two black-and-white fur balls just like in the zoo.
They're both very nice, and they're warm as can be.
But sometimes they tickle my feet when they sneeze!

Two snuggling ducks and two pandas that sneeze,
They're perfect to have, so at night I don't freeze.
But who snuck them past Mother and our lazy dog, Fred?
It's those *bunnies* who also end up on my bed!

Two bunnies as white as a new Christmas snow,
They sit on my stomach, which makes quite a show.
They're not heavy enough to push out all the air,
It's just for some reason they think I'm a chair!

So now when it's late and I'm all fast asleep,
I curl up with ducks, pandas, bunnies, and sheep.
Is my closet now empty? Is the picture complete?
Not without those two *kitties*, so soft and so sweet!

Two kitties who love to sleep on my bed,
Who purr-r-r in my ears and curl up by my head.
And if that's not enough, they say anything goes,
And let two little *puppies* lick me on the nose!

"Enough!" you might say. And I think you'd be right.
After all, all those animals make quite a sight!

But there's still one more friend, and we all really love her,
It's a *pony* named Gert, who must think she's my mother.
She stays up all night to guard me and the others.
And she's always right there if I kick off my covers.

I'll admit it, it's true; I won't fuss or fight.
I used to be scared of my closet at night.
But with ducks, pandas, rabbits, cats, dogs, and a horse,
Bedtime isn't something Mom and Dad have to force.

I put on my plaid jammies and brush all my teeth.
I comb out my hair and put soap on my cheeks,
Say "lay me down" prayers and hug Oscar, my sheep,
Then wait for my friends to come out when I sleep.

But there is just one thing that I wish wouldn't be.
Something I wish didn't happen to me.
Each morning, the first thing I happen to see,

Is how messy my hair is from ducks sleeping with me!

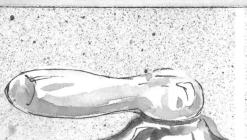

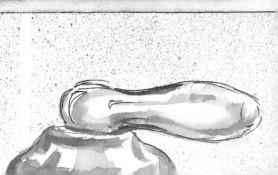